GREEN ARROW

₱OUNDS
OF VIOLENCE

KEVIN SMITH
Writer

PHIL HESTER
Penciller

ANDE PARKS
Inker

JAMES SINCLAIR
Colorist

SEAN KONOT
Letterer

MATT WAGNER
Original Covers

GREEN ARROW

SOUNDS
OF VIOLENCE

DAN DIDIO
VP-Editorial

BOB SCHRECK
Editor-original series

BOB GREENBERGER
Senior Editor-collected edition

ROBBIN BROSTERMAN
Senior Art Director

PAUL LEVITZ
President & Publisher

GEORG BREWER
VP-Design & Retail Product Development

RICHARD BRUNING
VP-Creative Director

PATRICK CALDON
Senior VP-Finance & Operations

CHRIS CARAMALIS
VP-Finance

TERRI CUNNINGHAM
VP-Managing Editor

ALISON GILL
VP-Manufacturing

LILLIAN LASERSON
Senior VP & General Counsel

DAVID MCKILLIPS
VP-Advertising

JOHN NEE
VP-Business Development

CHERYL RUBIN
VP-Licensing & Merchandising

BOB WAYNE
VP-Sales & Marketing

*Comic-book creators are a delusional lot.
At least I know I am.*

I've been laboring under the pretense that the comic-buying public — that's you — wouldn't start forming an opinion of my work until it became halfway presentable. I believed that I could fire some sort of imaginary starting gun on my career, letting all of you know that I was finally ready to be seen and judged.

And of course, as my work grew and improved over the last 15 years that point crept closer and closer in time. When I was 21 I was not yet embarrassed by my work for some of the smallest publishers and fanzines. In my 20s I expected those works to be forgotten and only my fledgling efforts with major publishers to be official. As I entered my 30s, by the time a job left my drawing table and made it into print, it was old enough to disavow. I've fired that starting gun so many times now that I'm out of ammo, hoping against hope that you kind people would forget my most awkward, amateurish efforts, and only latch on to work no more than 18 months old.

Kevin Smith shattered that delusion. When Bob Schreck asked me to collaborate with Kevin, first on *Clerks* and then on GREEN ARROW, my first response was, "Of course!" — then, a few seconds later, "Why me?"

Because, in case you folks haven't noticed, I'm no Neal Adams, or Mike Grell, or Rodolfo Damaggio, or Don Newton, or Trevor Von... you get the picture. I'm not exactly a normal Green Arrow artist. That didn't seem to matter to Kevin or Bob. You see, Kevin turned out to be a fan of my run on SWAMP THING, a book I worked on with the lovely and talented

Mark Millar for about 30 issues when we were both in our early-to-mid-20s. Way, way behind my imaginary 18-month window. A brilliant run, to be sure, but not because of me — rather, in spite of me. In my opinion, the strength of Mark's writing pulled the book above the artwork it was mired in.

But that work stuck in Kevin's mind enough for him to want to work with me years later. I was shocked to learn that he even owned a piece of original art from that run.

That's when something I heard over 15 years ago, at my very first comic-book convention, finally made sense to me. It was the height of the black-and-white explosion of the mid-'80s, and if you could hold a pencil pointy side down you could get work. I was attending a panel consisting of the reigning comic-book intelligentsia deriding the quality of the writers and artists emerging at the time, myself among them. The great Will Eisner offered a word of caution. Of course I'm paraphrasing, and maybe the glare of Mr. Eisner's aura clouded my perception, but he pointed out that my generation of artists would be one of the first in history to have our work scrutinized from day one, ready or not. He informed the would-be arbiters of funny book aesthetics that the ugly ducklings of today would be their collaborators and partners in the near future.

It took me 15 years to realize it, but he was right. So you got to see me and Brian Bendis and Guy Davis and countless other artists of my generation grow up on the page in front of you. Some of that work is painful to us now, but we can't take it back, and hey, it looks like some of you even enjoyed it. And for me, at least some of it led to the most rewarding gig of my career to date, GREEN ARROW.

And since I'm unlikely to have a forum like this again, please indulge me as I express my gratitude toward the people I've worked with for the last couple of years.

Besides being my Dad's favorite comedic director, a genius screenwriter, and all around swell guy, Kevin Smith is a miracle worker. The evidence is there, people. He made GREEN ARROW a top ten book. GREEN ARROW. Not BATMAN, not SUPERMAN, not even AQUAMAN. *GREEN ARROW*. Imagine what he could do with something like JLA. But rest assured, I intend to test his powers. I'm pushing for our next collaboration to be a revival of Brother Power, The Geek. We'll see just how much juice the man has then!

His scripts have been a joy. I've been allowed to run rampant on the DC playground, playing with toys previously reserved for greater talents. I've read some of the funniest and most poignant scripts

before anyone but my editors, and believe me, the funniest stuff was in the panel descriptions and margins, never seen by the reading public. Thanks for bringing me along on this ride, Kevin.

Nothing makes me happier than to hear the phrase "Hester and Parks." Although we shouldn't be mentioned in the same breath, ballpark, or universe as such great penciller/inker tandems as Kirby and Sinnott, Colan and Palmer, Miller and Janson, just to be known by that same nomenclature is the proudest achievement of my career. Thanks for saving my hide on every page, Anj.

Sean Konot remains the single most enthusiastic and stylistically satisfying letterer I've been privileged to work with. Guy Major and James Sinclair have transformed the messes we've laid in their laps into work of the highest quality with virtually no turnaround time at all. Thanks to all you guys for making us look like pros.

What can I say about the long-suffering Nachie Castro and his successor Morgan Dontanville? They did the heavy lifting every day on this book. It's impossible to imagine GREEN ARROW without them. The same goes to DC's unparalleled Production Department, and Bob Greenberger for putting this volume together.

Thanks also to Scott McCullar and those frequenting the various Green Arrow message boards for invaluable research and support. Hope we did you proud!

Finally, Bob Schreck. He's been manning the great

machine that is the comics industry for years, trying with more success than all but a few to steer this behemoth in the right direction. Look at some of the finest work of the last few decades and you'll see him behind the scenes. Talk with the most respected creators and you'll hear him counted as friend and advisor. Look for a group of laughing pros and fans alike at any convention and you'll find him at the head of the table.

Like many artists in this business, I've felt his presence before even meeting the man. He's been lurking at the edges of my career since the beginning, always looking for the right project to send my way. I'll always be in his debt, not just for GREEN ARROW but for the earlier jobs, the safe havens he carved out for me in which to develop my unique voice and earn a living. So, a dedication of sorts — this book, like so many others, could not exist without you.

One last thanks to the people reading this book. Thanks for hanging around long enough to make Green Arrow an important character again. I hope you enjoy this collection half as much as we enjoyed putting it together. If, for some reason, this book is your first exposure to Green Arrow, please drop by the monthly title some time. We're still having just as much fun.

Remember that starting gun? Well, it's gone for good now. I fired it for the last time when GREEN ARROW #1 hit the stands.

— Phil Hester
Somewhere in Iowa
January 8, 2003

BEEP! BEEP! BEEP! BEEP! BEEP!

SPEEDY!

KEVIN SMITH- Writer
PHIL HESTER- Penciller
ANDE PARKS- Inker
JAMES SINCLAIR- Colorist
SEAN KONOT- Letterer
BOB SCHRECK- Editor
NACHIE CASTRO- Assistant

THEY DON'T WAIT FOR SOMEONE *ELSE* TO LIGHT A FIRE...

...UNDER THEIR...

UH-OH...

MIA! WE'VE GOTTA HAVE A LITTLE TALK...

A CROSSBOW?!

STAR CITY YOUTH CENTER

ONE OF THOSE *HUNTRESS*-LOOKING JOBS.

AND SHE ACTUALLY *SAID* SHE WANTS YOU TO TRAIN HER AS THE NEW *SPEEDY?*

THAT'S WHAT SHE SAID.

LESS TALKIN', MORE PUDDIN'.

SORRY, LITTLE MAN.

HEY, FRANKIE-- WHAT DO WE *SAY* WHEN CONNOR HANDS US PUDDING?

THANKS, TIGER WOODS!

"TIGER WOODS"?

YEAH, I GET THAT A LOT.

SO, WHAT'D YOU TELL MIA ABOUT BEING SPEEDY?

Panel 3:
I DIDN'T KNOW *WHAT* TO SAY, SO I TOLD HER WE'D TALK ABOUT IT LATER.

HOW OLD IS SHE AGAIN?

FIFTEEN, SIXTEEN, MAYBE.

Panel 4:
YOU GOING TO TRAIN HER?

ARE YOU NUTS? SHE'S A KID!

YOUNG JUSTICE IS MADE UP OF "KIDS," AND THEY SEEM TO DO OKAY.

THE TITANS WERE "KIDS" ONCE, TOO, IF I REMEMBER CORRECTLY.

Panel 5:
Y'KNOW, YOU'RE A FAT LOAD'A *HELP.*

FACE IT, OLD TIMER-- YOU'RE A *YOUTH MAGNET.* YOU'VE ALWAYS SURROUNDED YOURSELF WITH YOUNG-STERS.

I MEAN, LOOK AT *THIS* PLACE. YOU COULD'VE HANDED IT OVER TO THE *CITY* TO RUN, BUT NO-- YOU JUST *HAD* TO KEEP IT GOING YOURSELF.

Panel 6:
WHAT ELSE WAS I GOING TO DO WITH THAT SICK OLD MAN'S BLOOD MONEY? AT LEAST HERE IT DOES SOME GOOD.

YOU KEEP TELLING YOURSELF THAT'S THE ONLY REASON YOU'RE SHOVELING OUT PUDDING TO GRADE-SCHOOLERS, POP. THE REST OF US KNOW BETTER.

AND WHAT IS IT THAT THE *REST OF YOU* THINK YOU KNOW?

THAT YOU'RE A **WANNABE-DAD**, DAD.

WHY DON'T YOU BEAT IT ALREADY? GO FIND YOUR-SELF A NICE GIRL TO SETTLE DOWN WITH?

TAKE YOUR OWN ADVICE, OLLIE.

AND WHAT'S **THAT** SUPPOSED TO MEAN?

FIGURE IT OUT... ...LANCE-LOVER.

SEE YOU TONIGHT.

Kid's got a point.

Not just about my paternal instincts, but about Dinah.

What're you afraid of, Beard-Boy? That she doesn't want you the way you want her anymore? That maybe there's been a gallon too much of the ol' water under the proverbial bridge?

I had the courage to walk out of Heaven, but I don't have the sack enough to pick up the phone and call my ex.

Typical Ollie.

I've been "back" for two weeks now, and I still haven't called her.

She probably understands, though... right? I mean, I *did* just return from the dead. Spending a little quality time with the kid I never got to know before warranted at *least* a week.

But that doesn't explain why I didn't call her last week.

Or this week, yet.

C'MON-- YOU'VE BRAVED FAR WORSE THAN THIS.

YEAH...

OH, HELLO, MISTER "DO-AS-I-SAY-NOT-AS-I-DO."

YOU'RE LATE.

DOCK ME.

SO, WHO'RE YOU TALKING TO?

NOBODY.

YOU READY TO TAKE OVER? I'VE GOTTA GO HOME AND GRAB A SHOWER BEFORE I GO OUT TONIGHT.

WHY BOTHER SHOWERING IF YOU'RE JUST GONNA GET ALL SWEATED-UP AGAIN BUSTING CRIMINALS ALL NIGHT?

JUST BECAUSE I BRING 'EM TO JUSTICE DOESN'T MEAN I GOTTA SMELL LIKE 'EM.

SO, I TAKE IT WE'RE NOT GONNA FINISH THIS MORNING'S CONVERSATION?

WE'LL DO IT TOMORROW MORNING.

MEANTIME, MAKE SURE YOU DO YOUR DISHES TONIGHT.

I GET HOME AGAIN TOMORROW MORNING AND I FIND ANY DISHES IN THAT SINK, YOU'RE WAKING UP TO A BED FULL'A ICE WATER.

YOU ALWAYS GONNA BE THIS EVASIVE?

DISHES, MIA.

YESSIR, YOUR ROYAL HIGHNESS.

JERK.

I HEARD THAT.

THE KID'S RIGHT. THAT WAS SOME NICE SHOOTING.

SEE? I *TOLD* YOU I WAS READY.

SO WHEN CAN I GO OUT WITH YOU GUYS?

YOU *CAN'T*.

WHY *NOT*?! YOU SAID YOUR-SELF-- MY SHOOTING'S PRETTY GOOD!

SIT DOWN, MIA.

I DON'T *GET* YOU. YOU OBVIOUSLY *WANT* A PARTNER.

NO-- I DON'T.

SO WHAT'S *CONNOR*? YOUR PIMP?

I'M JUST SPENDING SOME QUALITY TIME WITH CONNOR. AND, YES-- HE HAS BEEN *HELPFUL*.

HELPFUL?! WITHOUT HIM, *YOU'D* BE STANLEY DOVER, AND *I'D* BE *DEAD* RIGHT NOW!

TRUE.

BUT I'D LIKE TO THINK THERE'S MORE FOR HIM IN LIFE THAN JUST MIXING IT UP WITH STREET-LEVEL LOONIES AND THEIR COSTUMED COUNTERPARTS.

SO TELL *HIM*, BUT WHAT'S THAT GOT TO DO WITH *ME*?

I DON'T WANT TO TRAIN YOU TO TAKE HIS PLACE.

WHY THE HELL NOT?

FOR THE SAME REASON.

YOU'VE GOT YOUR *WHOLE LIFE* AHEAD OF YOU. PUTTING ON SOME TIGHTS AND DUKING IT OUT WITH THE DREGS OF SOCIETY ISN'T SOMETHING I RECOMMEND FOR KIDS.

RIGHT. BECAUSE ARSENAL WAS, LIKE, *FORTY-SIX* WHEN *HE* WAS SPEEDY.

KEVIN SMITH- WRITER
PHIL HESTER- PENCILS
ANDE PARKS- INKS
SEAN KONOT- LETTERS
JAMES SINCLAIR- COLORS & SEPS
BOB SCHRECK- EDITOR
NACHIE CASTRO- ASST. EDITOR

YEAH-- IT'S A REGULAR BRAWL-FOR-ALL IN HERE.

SHOULD I CHECK THE AIR DUCTS FOR JOKER-GAS?

Uh.... HELLO?

NAH. ME AN' BIG BIRD WERE JUST BUSTING ON THE GHOUL.

DO IT, OLIVER. DO YOUR BATMAN FOR DINAH.

"I TEND TO EXPECT THE UNEXPECTED."

HAHAHAHA! YOU EVEN-- YOU DID THE CAPE THIS TIME!

HE'S LIKE LINUS AND HIS BLANKET WITH THAT CAPE.

YOU WANT I SHOULD GET TED DOWN HERE TO BREAK THEM UP BEFORE THEY REALLY HURT EACH OTHER?

GO PRACTICE YOUR ROD-HANDLING.

FUNNY-- THAT'S WHAT I WAS GONNA TELL YOU BEFORE YOU LEFT FOR YOUR BIG DATE.

BOY, I MISSED YOU, CARTER! I NEVER THOUGHT I'D SAY THAT, BUT IT'S TRUE.

YOU'RE A GOOD EGG.

Heh.

AND THE *BIRD* CRACKS CONTINUE.

YOU KNOW, OLIVER-- THE ANCIENT EGYPTIANS HAD A *WORD* FOR PEOPLE LIKE YOU.

OH, YEAH? WHAT'S THAT?

"SCHMUCK."

HAHAHAHAHA!

Uh... OLIVER?

HAHAHAHAHAHA!

HEE-HEE...

YEAH?

OH, LORD, MY SIDES HURT...

WHY AREN'T YOU IN YOUR *CIVVIES*...?

IT SHOWED, DIDN'T IT? SHE'S HIP TO MY BULL, ISN'T SHE?

YOU'RE OVERREACTING, OLIVER.

NOPE. SHE KNOWS. SHE KNOWS I'M A NERVOUS WRECK ABOUT TAKING HER OUT. FEEL HOW CLAMMY I AM, FER CRYIN' OUT LOUD!

YOU ARE RATHER SWEATY.

OH, MAN, I KNEW I WASN'T READY FOR THIS YET.

NONSENSE! YOU'RE READY.

IT'S JUST...

I MEAN, THERE'S SO MUCH TO MAKE UP FOR. SO MUCH TO SAY.

BUT I WANT TO SKIP ALL THAT AND GET BACK TO THE WAY WE WERE BEFORE.

THEY DO LIKE TO MAKE IT DIFFICULT, DON'T THEY?

WE CAN TRAVEL ACROSS TIME AND TRAVERSE THE BORDERS OF DEATH FOR THEM...

...AND WE'RE STILL AT THEIR MERCY.

A WORD, THOUGH, OLIVER...

DINAH'S BEEN THROUGH A GREAT DEAL THIS YEAR, FROM WHAT I UNDERSTAND. SHE'S IN NO SHAPE TO MAKE ANY MONUMENTAL DECISIONS.

YOUR POINT?

TREAT HER WITH CARE AND CAUTION, RESPECT HER BOUNDARIES, DO NOT RUSH HER INTO A RELATIONSHIP JUST YET.

NO WORRIES THERE, HALL-Y...

SEE THESE HANDS...?

ARE THEY ANYWHERE *NEAR* YOUR SIDE OF THE TABLE?

I THINK NOT.

SO, BESIDES THE GENOCIDAL MANIAC, ARE THERE ANY OTHER NOTEWORTHY MEN YOU'VE BEEN... *SPENDING TIME* WITH?

TWENTY-*NINE*.

YEAH, BUT MY MOM ALWAYS SAID TO WATCH OUT FOR ANY GUY WHO CAN NOCK TWENTY-SIX ARROWS A MINUTE.

DOCTOR MIDNIGHT.

GET OUTTA HERE...

I'M NOT KIDDING.

THE GUY WITH THE *OWL*?

EW.

WHAT, "*EW*"?

WELL, I MEAN...

HE HANGS OUT WITH AN *OWL*.

DO I DETECT A NOTE OF *JEALOUSY*, MISTER QUEEN?

YOU'RE DAMN SKIPPY YOU DO.

I DON'T LIKE *ANYONE* LAYIN' A HAND ON *MY GIRL*.

YOU'LL HAVE TO EXCUSE ME FOR NOT BUSTING OUT WITH THE "A" MATERIAL, BUT I'M ONLY POPPING IN TO GRAB SOME TAKE-OUT.

PLEASE DEPOSIT ALL WALLETS, PURSES, GOLD, DIAMONDS, AND ANY OTHER VARIOUS VALUABLES INTO THE DOGGY BAGS, AND WE'LL BE OUT OF YOUR HAIR QUICKER THAN YOU CAN SAY...

HEY, JACKASS!

WELL...

I *WAS* GONNA SAY, IS THAT YOUR *FINAL ANSWER?* A DATED REFERENCE, I KNOW.

THREE AND THREE.

AND I'LL EVEN GIVE YOU ALEX TREBEK OVER THERE.

YOU'RE TOO KIND.

HERE'S AN *EASY* ONE.

WHAT'S FULL OF HOLES AND RED AND--

KRAK!

46

SHE CAN BE CREDITED WITH TWELVE ARRESTS IN HER FLEDGLING CAREER, THUS FAR.

SHE'S THWARTED SIX MUGGINGS, THREE B. AND E'S, TWO INSTANCES OF ROAD RAGE, AND ONE ATTEMPT AT GRAFFITI TO THE LIBERTY BELL.

SHE CALLS HERSELF... VIRAGO.

THE NAME'S MEANT TO BE IRONIC-- AS VIRAGO IS FAR FROM A HAG OR A SHREW.

NO! SOMEONE, PLEASE HELP!

ACTUALLY, SHE'S QUITE THE LOOKER.

PROBLEM IS, SHE'S NOT LOOKING...

...BEFORE SHE LEAPS.

PAF!

SPFF!

SKKKKRRRRREEEEEEEEEEE!

SKKKKRRRRREEEEEE!

AAAHHHHH!!!

AAAHHHHH!!!

SKKKKRRRRREEEEEE!

SKKRREEEE!

OW! WHAT THE HECK IS GOING ON?! IS THAT DINAH?!

SOMEONE MUST'VE BREACHED THE MANOR! C'MON! SHE NEEDS OUR HELP!

HER SONIC CRY'S AFFECTING MY STABILITY!

THANKS.

YOU CAN GET UP NOW.

BOY... YOU GOT SOME *BALLS* ON YOU.

UM...

GET IT?

WHOOOSH!

WHOOOSH!

"GET IT"?
YES, YES, I "GET IT".
BUT WILL YOU BE DOING THE SAME ANY TIME SOON?

DON'T BET ON IT, QUEEN.

WHOOSH!
WHOOSH!
WHOOSH!

SLAM!

SHE'S CRAZY ABOUT ME.

HARRISBURG, PENNSYLVANIA WILL WAKE UP TO GOOD NEWS THIS MORNING...

SHE'S FREE OF MENACE.

FOR NEARLY TWO WEEKS, A WOULD-BE SUPER-VILLAIN CALLING HIMSELF "PANACEA" HAUNTED HER NORMALLY QUIET STREETS, KILLING NINE LAWYERS IN WHAT HE TERMED A "PUBLIC SERVICE."

BUT AT FOUR THIRTY A.M., PANACEA'S REIGN OF TERROR WAS ENDED BY HARRISBURG'S TRUE PUBLIC SERVANT.

HE CALLS HIMSELF BUCKEYE.

IN THE SIX MONTHS SINCE HIS FIRST 'BURG APPEARANCE, HE'S BROUGHT IN A CHILD MOLESTER, PREVENTED SIXTEEN MUGGINGS, AND CLOSED DOWN THE BURGEONING DRUG TRADE.

THE LOCAL PRESS HAS HAILED HIS ARRIVAL, BUT THEY'RE ALSO PUZZLED BY HIS SEEMINGLY INAPPROPRIATE CHOICE OF HERO NAME.

WHAT THEY DON'T KNOW IS THAT EVEN THOUGH HARRISBURG IS HIS NEW BASE OF OPERATIONS, BUCKEYE IS TOO ATTACHED TO HIS OHIO-BORN ALIAS TO ALTER IT.

YOU SEE, BUCKEYE'S HOME STATE OF OHIO IS WHERE HE MET HIS WIFE.

AND THE ONLY THING BUCKEYE LOVES MORE THAN FIGHTING CRIME...

... IS HIS WIFE.

I GOT HIM, BABE. I GOT THE BASTARD.

MEG?

I'M HOME.

drip!

YOU SHOULD'VE SEEN HIM, TOO.

JUST A WIMPY LITTLE SONOVA-SO-AND-SO.

drip!

SOUNDS LIKE THE SHOWER'S STILL DRIPPING, HUNH? I'LL FIX THAT WHEN I WAKE UP.

JUST WANNA SEE IF THERE'S ANYTHING ON THE NEWS ABOUT LAST NIGHT.

drip!

CLIK!

CLIK.

drip!

drip!

drip!

D'JOU SAY SOMETHIN'? MEG?

BABE?

...AND WAS PROMPTLY ARRESTED BY AUTHORITIES.

CHIEF OF POLICE ANDERS HAD THIS TO SAY ABOUT BUCKEYE'S CAPTURE OF PANACEA...

"I'LL GO ON RECORD AS SAYING BUCKEYE IS WELCOME HERE IN HARRISBURG-- VIGILANTE OR NOT."

"I JUST WISH HE'D CHANGE THAT NAME OF HIS."

62

IF I HADN'T SHOWN UP, WHAT?

HM?

YOU SAID IF I HADN'T SHOWN UP WHEN I DID...

IF I HADN'T SHOWN UP, WHAT?

I DON'T KNOW, THAT'S JUST A THING I'VE HEARD PEOPLE SAY.

THAT INCOMPLETE-THOUGHT-THING.

WHAT?

WHAT'S THE STORY WITH YOU AND GIRLS, ANYWAY?

YOU'RE NOT TRYING TO HAVE "THE TALK" WITH ME, ARE YOU?

THEY GIVE YOU "THE TALK" UP AT THE ASHRAM?

HOW CAN YOU HAVE "THE TALK" WHEN BARELY ANYONE TALKS, PERIOD?

SPEAKING OF WHICH, HOW'D YOUR DATE GO?

DON'T ASK. YOU PATROL LAST NIGHT?

ACROSS TOWN, AT THE BROWNSTONE...

YOU'RE WATCHING K-STAR. NUMBER ONE IN STAR CITY...

A HERO FALLS IN STAR CITY, WE'LL HAVE THE LATEST FROM STAR CITY MEMORIAL ON GREEN ARROW'S FIGHT FOR LIFE.

WHAT?!

AND DID THE MERCS TAKE OUT THE DEVILS TONIGHT?

WE'LL TAKE YOU LIVE TO GAME FIVE OF THE STANLEY CUP AT STAR ARENA. ALL THIS, AND MORE, ON K-STAR ACTION NEWS.

Not when I was just getting to know him...

OLLIE!

OH, MY GOD! THE STUPID NEWS SAID YOU WERE--

NOT ME.

CONNOR... JESUS-- NO...

I CAN'T STAND HERE AND WATCH THIS ANYMORE.

YOU TWO STAY WITH HIM.

BUT, CONNOR...

...IS IN GOOD HANDS, I CAN'T HELP HIM NOW.

OLIVER, WAIT! WHERE ARE YOU GOING?

TO FIND THE SONOVABITCH WHO DID THIS TO MY SON.

MISTER... ARROW?

GET OUT OF MY WAY!

IS HE GOING TO LIVE?

THAT DEPENDS ON YOU, SIR, HE'S LOST A LOT OF BLOOD, AND HE'S GONNA NEED A TRANSFUSION.

ARE YOU THE BIOLOGICAL FATHER?

OLIVER!

OLIVER, RIGHT, I WASN'T SURE WHAT TO CALL YOU.

I HAVE AN UPDATE ON CONNOR.

YES!

THEN WE'VE GOTTA GET YOU INTO THE O.R. IMMEDIATELY!

HE ADAMS HOTEL, FOUR BLOCKS AWAY IN DOWNTOWN STAR...

... HERE, NOW, WITH MORE DETAILS FROM STAR MEMORIAL, IS MITCH INGRAM.

86

FLUSH!

FLUSH.

GRANT, WE'VE JUST RECEIVED WORD THAT IT'S NOT THE RECENTLY RETURNED GREEN ARROW WHO'S UNDERGOING EMERGENCY SURGERY FOLLOWING A GUN-SHOT WOUND...

...THE ELDER GREEN ARROW STILL HASN'T LEFT THE BUILDING, SO WE CAN ONLY ASSUME HOW DIRE THE SITUATION INSIDE IS FOR STAR CITY'S GREATEST HERO AND HIS YOUNG COUNTERPART.

HM...?

IT'S THE YOUNGER GREEN ARROW WHO SOURCES TELL US WAS CARRIED INTO THE EMERGENCY ROOM BY THE OLDER GREEN ARROW, SUFFERING FROM WHAT ONE EYEWITNESS DESCRIBED AS A "FATAL-LOOKING HEAD-SHOT."

NO WORD YET ON THE YOUNG HERO'S CURRENT CONDITION, BUT SOURCES TELL US THAT AS HE'S NOT A META-HUMAN, THE NEXT HOUR IN SURGERY IS GOING TO BE CRUCIAL.

REPORTING FROM STAR CITY MEMORIAL HOSPITAL, I'M MITCH INGRAM.

IS THE YOUNGER ONE YOUR DAUGHTER?

KINDA... NOT REALLY... I ONLY HAVE... THE BOY...

WHO'S VERY LUCKY YOU WERE HERE TONIGHT.

WE HAD A RUN ON *O POSITIVE* YESTERDAY WITH ANOTHER SURGERY, AND THE REPLENISHMENT STOCK HASN'T COME IN YET.

IF YOU WEREN'T HERE FOR HIM TONIGHT...

... WHO KNOWS WHAT MIGHT'VE HAPPENED.

WHAT THE HELL...?

THAT SOUNDED LIKE...

... A GUNSHOT.

HELLO...? NURSE? WHAT'S--

OH, MY GOD...!

BLAM.

TOWER

GOD... BILL AND MARTIN...

I MEAN... THEY BOTH HAVE WIVES AND KIDS...

IT COULD'VE BEEN ME...

DOC-- KEEP IT TOGETHER, I NEED YOU SHARP.

IS THE LADY IN BLACK ALL RIGHT?

SHE'S BRUISED AND CUT, BUT IT'S NOTHING LIFE-THREATENING.

SHE'S SURVIVED A LOT WORSE. TAKE HER OUT OF HERE AND CLEAN HER UP, PLEASE.

YOU OKAY UP THERE, MIA?

I'LL LIVE.

IS CONNOR OKAY?

HE WAS BEFORE SOMEONE SHOT HIM IN THE HEAD LAST NIGHT.

GO OUT THERE AND DEBRIEF THE COPS, THE STAFF, WHOEVER, BUT TELL 'EM TO STAY AWAY FROM THE O.R.

TELL 'EM THERE'S A SITUATION IN HERE, AND ME AND A LEAGUER ARE HANDLING IT.

A "LEAGUER"?

THE BLACK CANARY. NAME-DROPPING THE JLA WILL BUY US SOME TIME.

TELL 'EM NO MATTER WHAT THEY HEAR, THEY'VE GOTTA STAY AWAY FROM THE O.R., BECAUSE WE'RE TRYING TO CONTAIN ONE OF THOSE SUPER-VILLAINS ONLY THE JUSTICE LEAGUE CAN HANDLE.

SO LIE BIG?

SOMETHING LIKE THAT.

GO.

GONE!

"I'D NEVER SEEN ANYTHING LIKE IT."

TWO WEEKS LATER...

IT WAS JUST... IT WAS JUST INSANE.

AND AFTER ALL THAT, HE JUST...

...DISAPPEARED?

"WHEN I GOT DOWNSTAIRS...

"...HE WAS GONE,

"HE'D KILLED SOMEONE IN THE PARKING GARAGE AND TOOK THEIR CAR.

"THEY FOUND THE CAR A COUPLE MILES AWAY, BUT NO SIGN OF HIM."

Phil Hester and Ande Parks have collaborated together for years and enjoy the process of creating new characters. On this and the following pages, we present a sampling of their page designs and character concepts.

The Green Arrow model sheet first appeared in *Wizard Magazine*.

Kevin Smith as Green Arrow was done for a magazine.

The Green Arrow and Demon piece was done on commission.

GREEN ARROW CHARACTER REDESIGN ROUGH #5 - LEATHER STRAPS

GREEN ARROW COSTUME REDESIGN SKETCH - 7 - STREAMLINED CLASSIC

GREEN ARROW CHARACTER REDESIGN 8 - SWASHBUCKLER

MY FAVORITE SO FAR! OR MAYBE NOT...

JUST A FEW ALTERATIONS TO CLASSIC THREADS.

A LITTLE MORE ERROL FLYNN. KINDA LIKE IT. LEATHER VEST, CAP, GLOVES, QUIVER. GOLD BUCKLES, SHOULDER EPAULETS.

A SAMPLE OF Phil's pencils and the finished Phil and Andy page.

Phil notes, "In the middle of Kevin's run we toyed with the idea of putting Mia in a Speedy costume and changing Ollie's costume. Neither came to pass."

KEVIN SMITH

In the few years since his entry into the indie film community, Kevin Smith has seen it all — from the surprise critical and commercial success he received for his debut film *Clerks* to the disappointing critical and commercial drubbing he took on his second outing, *Mallrats*. He caught a break on his third film, the critically hailed *Chasing Amy*, and managed not to get killed by the religious zealots over his fourth film, the comedic meditation *Dogma*. Thus not deterred, Smith advanced and has written and directed the fifth and final installment in his New Jersey Chronicles, *Jay and Silent Bob Strike Back*, released by Dimension Films in August 2001. His next film, *Jersey Girl*, will be released in the summer of 2003.

Along the way, Smith has also found time to make himself a nuisance by smearing his name all over the pop culture landscape. He collaborated with indie film guru John Pierson on his best-selling book *Spike, Mike, Slackers, and Dykes*. He's published the screenplays for all four of his films. He's written comic books featuring not only his own characters (*Clerks* and *Jay and Silent Bob*), but other characters as well (the award-winning *Daredevil* at Marvel Comics, and the award-winning GREEN ARROW at DC comics). With his View Askew partner, Scott Mosier, he's also produced four low-budget, first-film efforts, including Bryan Johnson's Lion Gate release, *Vulgar*. Smith and Mosier also co-executive produced the Academy Award-winning *Good Will Hunting*, starring View Askew stalwarts (and then unknowns) Matt Damon and Ben Affleck.

Besides *Mallrats*, Smith has survived other humbling "creative" experiences which he inexplicably has failed to suppress — such as his ill-fated *Superman Lives* screenplay for Warner Bros., and his animated series version of *Clerks* for ABC primetime, which the network unceremoniously cancelled after airing only two episodes.

But, but, but, Smith was one of the first filmmakers to venture into cyberspace, establishing the insanely popular View Askewniverse website (www.viewaskew.com) in the mid-nineties. And if the film thing doesn't pan out, he does own his own comic-book store — Jay and Silent Bob's Secret Stash, in beautiful downtown Red Bank, New Jersey.

As for the hood ornaments he's collected, there's plenty of tin to go around: the Filmmaker's Trophy at Sundance for *Clerks*; the Prix de la Jeunesse and the International Critic's Week Award at the Cannes Film Festival, also for *Clerks*; The Independent Spirit Award for Best Screenplay for *Chasing Amy*; and a Humanitas Award for *Good Will Hunting*. For his writing in the comics field, Smith has received a Harvey Award, a Wizard Fan Award, and an Eagle Award.

Yet at the end of the day, the two titles Smith touts most proudly are "husband" and "father." He married his wife Jennifer in April of 1999, and celebrated the birth of their daughter, Harley Quinn, in June of that same year (you do the math).

PHIL HESTER

Phil lives in rural Iowa with his wife and two children. He began working in comics while attending The University of Iowa, from which he graduated with a BFA in drawing with minors in sculpture and painting. He has worked for nearly every comic-book publisher in the last 15 years and has been featured in over 300 issues.

Phil's past work includes SWAMP THING, DETECTIVE COMICS, *The Crow: Waking Nightmares*, *The Coffin* (writer), *The Wretch* ('96 Eisner Award nominee), THE CREEPER, *Ultimate Marvel Team-Up*, BRAVE OLD WORLD, *Fringe*, *Rust*, *Taboo*, *The Picture Taker* (writer), *Attitude Lad*, *Deadline USA*, *Negative Burn*, *Clerks: The Lost Scene* and lots, lots more.

His current and upcoming work includes: GREEN ARROW, *Deep Sleeper*, *Firebreather*, and *The Operation*.

He is nice and likes nice people.

ANDE PARKS

Born and raised in Kansas, Ande Parks has been employed in the glamorous world of comic-book inking for over a decade, lending his talents to such titles as SUPERMAN, WONDER WOMAN, and CATWOMAN. Often teamed with his longtime friend Phil Hester, he has won acclaim for his bold, graphic style. Parks has also created his own characters, Uncle Slam and Fire Dog. He is currently continuing his work on GREEN ARROW and is writing a gangster graphic novel. He lives in Kansas with his lovely wife and daughter.

THE STARS OF THE
DC UNIVERSE
CAN ALSO BE FOUND IN THESE BOOKS:

TO FIND MORE COLLECTED EDITIONS AND MONTHLY COMIC BOOKS FROM DC COMICS,
CALL 1-888-COMIC BOOK FOR THE NEAREST COMICS SHOP OR GO TO YOUR LOCAL BOOK STORE.

Visit us at www.dccomics.com